The POKY LITTL
Special Spring Day

By Diane Muldrow, after Janette Sebring Lowrey,
author of *The Poky Little Puppy*

Illustrated by Sue DiCicco

A GOLDEN BOOK • NEW YORK

Copyright © 2021 by Penguin Random House LLC. All rights reserved.
Published in the United States by Golden Books, an imprint of Random House Children's Books,
a division of Penguin Random House LLC, 1745 Broadway, New York, NY 10019. Golden Books,
A Golden Book, A Little Golden Book, the G colophon, and the distinctive gold spine are
registered trademarks of Penguin Random House LLC. The Poky Little Puppy is a trademark
of Penguin Random House LLC.
rhcbooks.com
Educators and librarians, for a variety of teaching tools, visit us at RHTeachersLibrarians.com
Library of Congress Control Number: 2019946407
ISBN 978-0-593-12775-9 (trade) — ISBN 978-0-593-12776-6 (ebook)
Printed in the United States of America
10 9 8 7 6

One sunny morning, five little puppies went for a walk.

Through the meadow they went, down the road, over the bridge, and across the green grass, one right after the other. Along the way, they listened to the robins chirp.

"Look! The cherry tree is blooming!" cried the puppies. "Springtime is here!"

When they got to the top of the hill, they counted themselves: *one, two, three, four.* One little puppy wasn't there.

Now, where in the world is that poky little puppy? they wondered.

When they looked down at the bottom of the hill, there he was, barking at something on the next hill.

"I see something!" Poky called. "A bright yellow kite!"

The other puppies saw it, too.
Over the hill they ran, as fast as they could go.

They found a group of children laughing and playing, flying their colorful kites high in the air. The happy puppies chased after the kites— roly-poly, pell-mell, tumble-bumble!

When the children went home for lunch, the puppies counted themselves: *one, two, three, four.* One little puppy wasn't there.

Where in the world was the poky little puppy?

There he was, behind some pussy willows, sitting still as a stone.

"What in the world are you doing?" the puppies asked.

"I hear something!" said the poky little puppy.

The puppies listened, and they could hear it, too.

Neep, neep! Neep, neep!

"Oh!" Poky suddenly cried. Lots of tiny frogs were hopping here and there!

But there weren't only frogs in the pond. Some turtles swam up with their babies to look at the puppies! And soon a proud mama duck appeared with her little ducklings.

Quack! Quack!

Just then, it started to rain.

The frogs began to hop, hop, hop from one puddle to the next.

"*Whee!*" cried the puppies. They jumped—*kersplash!*—into the puddles after the frogs. What fun!

When the puppies shook off their wet fur, they counted themselves: *one, two, three, four.* One little puppy wasn't there.

They soon found Poky sniffing the air.
"What in the world are you doing?" they asked.
"I smell something!" said the poky little puppy.

The four little puppies began to sniff, and they
smelled it, too.
"Spring flowers!" they cried.

Around the bend they ran, as fast as they could go, until they came to a beautiful garden. There were pink hyacinths and white crocuses and yellow daffodils in bloom. Oh, how sweet and fresh they smelled!

But that wasn't all the puppies found.
"Butterflies!" they cried.

The butterflies flew away, but the puppies didn't mind. Zigging and zagging ahead of them were some bunnies with puffy white tails! The bunnies led the puppies into a farmyard that had a chicken coop full of fluffy yellow chicks.

After the puppies watched the chickens scratch
around in the dirt, they counted themselves: *one,
two, three, four.* One little puppy wasn't there.
Where was that poky little puppy *now*?
"I found something!" they heard Poky call.

It was a beautiful Easter egg!

"Hello, puppies!" said a little girl. "We're having an Easter egg hunt. See how many eggs you can find!"

Off the puppies ran, as fast as they could go, to find the hidden Easter eggs.

Soon they found *one, two, three, four, five* colorful eggs—and their little basket was full!

"Jump in, puppies," said the girl. "I'll take you home!"

"*Whee!*" said the puppies as they bounced and bumped along in the little red wagon.

That evening, as the sun went down,
the puppies ate their Easter eggs for dinner.
Then they curled up on their puppy pillows
to go to sleep.

But the poky little puppy was the last to fall asleep. He couldn't stop thinking about his breezy, showery, hoppy, flowery, special spring day.